This book is dedicated to my mom, grandma, and dad.
I would also like to say a special thank you to my closest supporters,
you know who you are.
You mean the world to me.

My name is Sasha and my favorite day of the week is Sunday
when I get to cook
with my grandma who I call Mama.

Rice

She shows me how to make recipes like rice and peas

and jerk chicken.

And today, we are making
Jamaican beef patties and veggie ones too!

Scallions

Thyme

Flour

Curry

Onion

Scotch bonnet pepper

While we cook, she tells me stories about growing up in Jamaica, and how she used to walk miles to get to school.
And even when I have a lot of questions, she answers all of them.

She shows me how to measure and mix,

and how to **stir** and **roll**.

1/4 Teaspoon

1/2 Teaspoon

1 Tablespoon

1 Teaspoon

Measuring

Mixing

Rolling

Stirring

Flour

Salt

Curry

Cumin

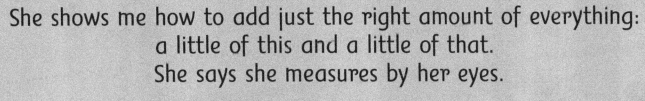

She shows me how to add just the right amount of everything:
a little of this and a little of that.
She says she measures by her eyes.

We add ingredients like garlic, curry,
and even scotch bonnet peppers.
But she chops those up because

they are extra spicy.

She tells me that the most important

ingredient when cooking is love.

And that full bellies make hearts happy
and stomachs smile.

Sometimes, we even play music and dance around the kitchen while we wait.

And even when there is a spill, she is patient with me.
And helps me clean it up.

The kitchen always smells so good
that everyone comes running.

But Mama makes them wash their hands
before they step foot into the kitchen.

When the food is almost ready, I help her put everything on the table

and make it look pretty.

Sundays are the **best** because
I get to wear my apron and spend time with
my grandma.

Sundays are the best because I get to make
hearts happy and stomachs **smile.**

CPSIA information can be obtained
at www.ICGtesting.com
Printed in the USA
LVHW071038021120
670440LV00004B/21